交响诗

铁道游击队

吕其明

Lü Qiming
RAILROAD GUERRILLA
SYMPHONIC POEM
SCORE
(1964)

总 谱

上海音乐出版社
SHANGHAI MUSIC PUBLISHING HOUSE

交响诗
《铁道游击队》

半个多世纪过去了，但我绝对忘不了我所经历过的抗日战争。那无数可歌可泣、令人赞颂的故事震撼着我的心灵，始终萦绕在我的脑际。铁道游击队，只是鲁南一支小小的游击队，他们在铁道线上"扒飞车、搞机枪、闯火车、炸桥梁，就像钢刀插入敌胸膛，打得鬼子魂飞胆丧"的英雄事迹，折射出中华民族不畏强暴、英勇奋战、不怕牺牲、保卫祖国的伟大民族精神。

乐曲为奏鸣曲式。以故事影片《铁道游击队》原创音乐为素材。音乐语言朴实无华，有着浓郁的乡土气息和地方色彩；抒发了革命战士"压倒一切敌人，而决不被敌人所屈服"的英雄气概，以及赶走侵略者、"人民的胜利就要来到"的必胜信念。

作者

About symphonic Poem "Railroad Guerilla"

Though more than half a century has past, I could not forget the War of Resistance against Japan I had experienced. I was deeply moved to song and tears by those countless, extolled stories and they remained in my brain. The railroad guerilla, a small guerilla in south Shandong, "climbed onto traveling trains, grabbed arms, intruded trains, and bombed bridges, acted as a steel sword cut in the enemies' chests, which made the enemies' souls out of their wits." Their heroic deeds refracted our great national spirit-defying brute force, fighting valiantly, fearing death not as well as protecting out nation.

The form of this symphony is sonata and it is based on the original music of the movie "Railroad Guerilla", the musical language is simple and unadorned, full of native flavor and local color, which expresses the revolutionary soldiers' heroic spirit of "overwhelming all enemies, and never submitting to them" with the belief of "people's victory will come soon" and their determination of driving intruders away as well.

Composer

乐队编制
Orchestra

短笛	Flauto Piccolo	Fi.Picc
长笛 (2支)	Flautt	Fl
双簧管 (2支)	Oboi	Ob
单簧管 (†B) (2支)	Claneti(†B)	Cl
低音单簧管 (†B)	Clarinetto basso	Cl.b.
大管 (2支)	Fagotti	Fag
圆号（F）(4支)	Corni	Cor
小号（†B）(3支)	Tromboni(†B)	Trbn
长号 (3支)	Tromboni	Trbn
大号	Tuba	Tuba
定音鼓 (4架)	Timpani	Timp
小军鼓	Tambuyo	Tamb
钗	Piatti	Piat.
大鼓	Gran Cassa	G.C.
大锣	Tam-Tam	Tam-t.
竖琴	Arpa	Arpa
第一小提琴	Violini	Vl.I
第二小提琴	Violini	Vl.II
中提琴	Viole	Vle
大提琴	Violoncelli	VC.
低音提琴	Contrabassi	Cb

铁道游击队
RAILROAD GUERILLA

吕 其 明
Lü Qiming

160
18
Picc.
Fl.
Ob.
Cl.
Cl. b.
Fag.
Cor.
Tr-be.
Tr-ni.
e
Tuba
Timp.
Piatti
Arpa.
rit.
mp
Vln. I
mf
mf
rit.
Vln. II
mp
p
Vla.
mp
p
Vc.
mp
mp
Cb.

228
27
28
Picc.
Fl.
Ob.
Cl.
Cl. b.
Fag.
Cor.
Tr-be.
Tr-ni.
e
Tuba
Timp.
Tamb
Piatti
Cassa
Vln. I
Vln. II
Vla.
Vc.
Cb.
mf
mp
p
f